For Timothy, Wyatt, and Maverick,
who make my heart whole
and inspire me beyond measure—
thank you

Published by Roaring Brook Press
Roaring Brook Press is a division of Holtzbrinck Publishing Holdings Limited Partnership
120 Broadway, New York, NY 10271 • mackids.com

Library of Congress Control Number: 2021916675
ISBN 978-1-250-76804-9

Our books may be purchased in bulk for promotional, educational, or business use.
Please contact your local bookseller or the Macmillan Corporate and Premium Sales Department
at (800) 221-7945 ext. 5442 or by email at MacmillanSpecialMarkets@macmillan.com.

First edition, 2022
Printed in China by Toppan Leefung Printing Ltd., Dongguan City, Guangdong Province

1   3   5   7   9   10   8   6   4   2

ABOUT THIS BOOK The illustrations for this book were created with pencil,
ink, watercolor, and acrylic, and combined and manipulated in Procreate and Photoshop.
This book was edited by Emily Feinberg and designed by Lisa Vega.
The production was supervised by Susan Doran, and the production editor was Allyson Floridia.
The text and display type was set in YWFT Absent Grotesque.

KITTY

rebecca jordan-glum

Roaring Brook Press
New York

"Don't worry about a thing," Granny said. "The cat will be just fine!"

Everything Granny needed to know was
written on a note taped to the fridge.

How convenient,
thought Granny.

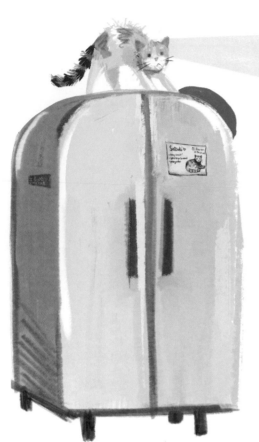

something frightened the cat,

which gave Granny quite a start.
The cat leaped one way,
Granny's glasses flew the other—

and the note
fluttered to the floor.

"Oh dear!" exclaimed Granny. "The ink is smudged."
She was relieved that she could still read the words.

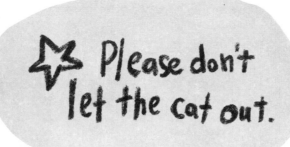

Well, that shouldn't be a problem, thought Granny.

But when she looked up, she saw the cat had already escaped!

So she grabbed the cat food and coaxed it back inside.

"My, what a big appetite you have!" Granny remarked.

"I'm feeling a bit peckish myself.
Time to make cupcakes," Granny said.

Kitty thought so, too.

When Granny wasn't looking,

Kitty stole a cupcake.

Granny was not pleased.

"Someone needs a bath!" she said.

Kitty was not pleased.

But after a good brushing,

Kitty was BEYOND pleased.

Granny spent the rest of the day
trying to keep Kitty out of trouble,
which wasn't easy.

Night fell.
Granny went to bed.

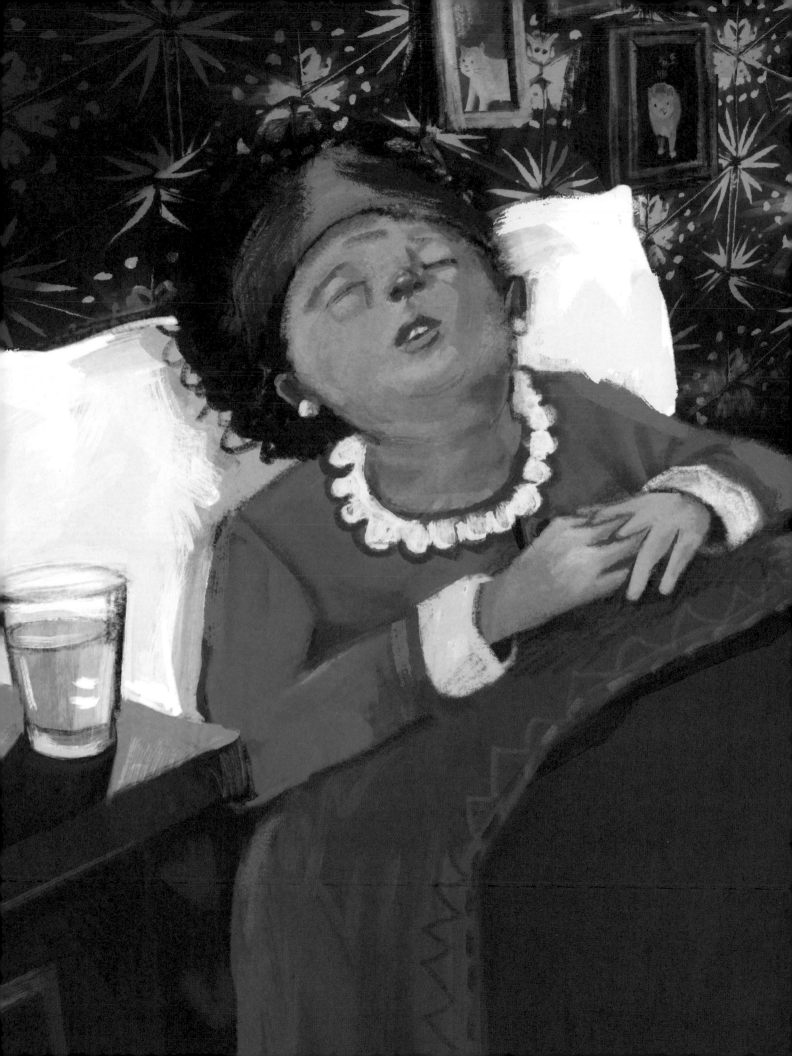

CRUNCH

NIBBLE

WHEEZE

SQUISH

THUNK

CRASH

Whooooosh

Kitty did not.

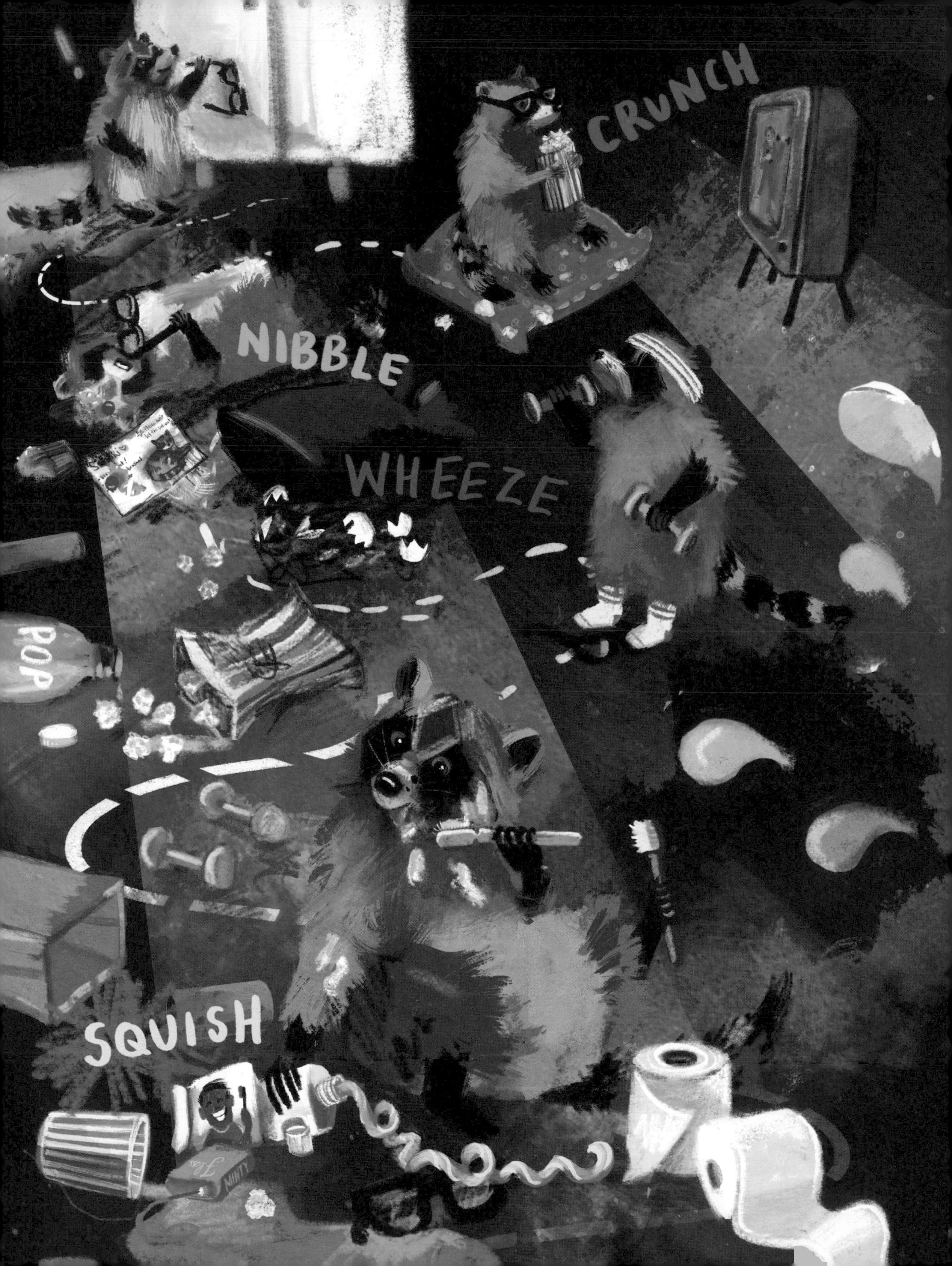
CRUNCH
NIBBLE
WHEEZE
POP
SQUISH
MINTY

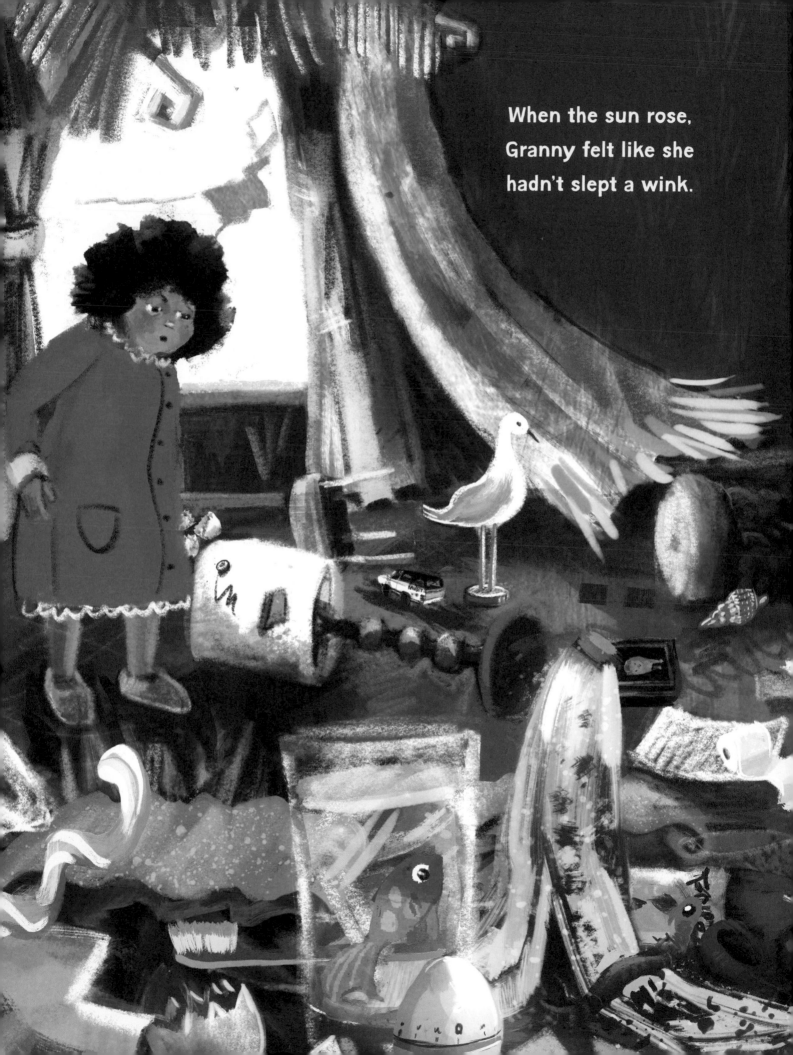

When the sun rose,
Granny felt like she
hadn't slept a wink.

Kitty had eventually gone to
bed—and never slept better.

And then the family
was home.

"It's a pity I can't stay," she muttered
as she dashed out the door.

"Kitty was a perfect angel!"
she shouted with only one thought . . .

Thank goodness I don't have a cat!